This book belongs to:

READY to RIDE

For my brother Christophe, who was there when my training wheels were taken off.
Thanks to David, for the spark.
Thanks to Servane, Camille, Anne-Claire, and Héloïse for their precious help.

Translated from the French by Vanessa Miéville

First published in the English language in 2018 by
words & pictures, an imprint of The Quarto Group.
6 Orchard Road
Suite 100
Lake Forest, CA 92630
T: +1 949 380 7510
F: +1 949 380 7575
www.QuartoKnows.com

A CIP record for the book is available from the Library of Congress.

ISBN: 978-1-91027-773-7

1 3 5 7 9 8 6 4 2

Manufactured in Dongguan, China TL012018

READY to RIDE

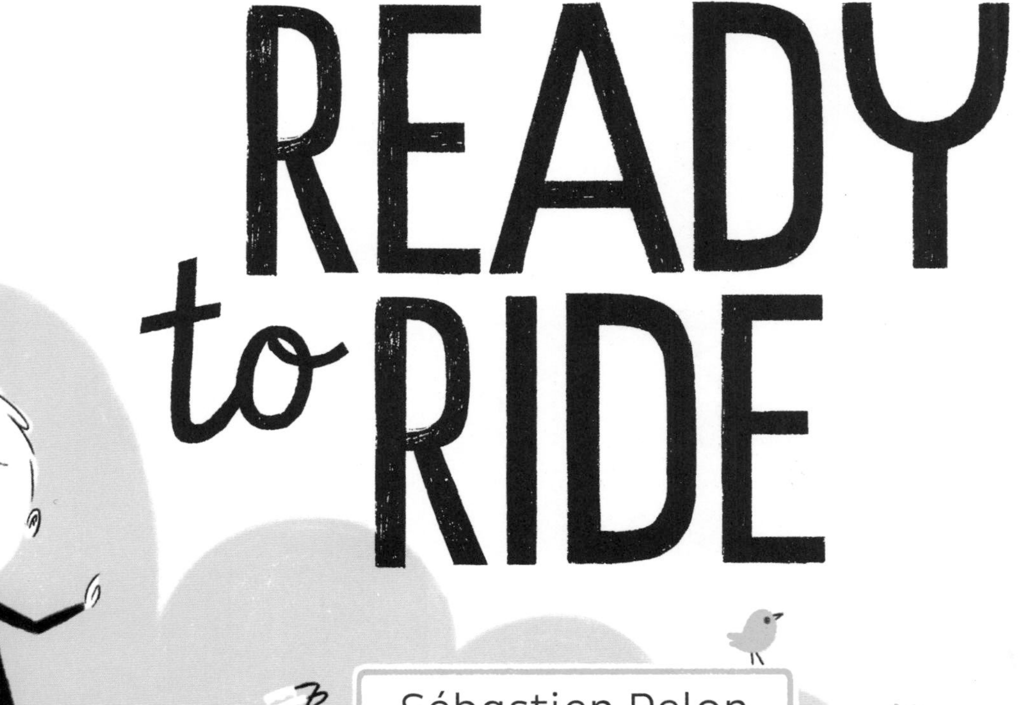

Sébastien Pelon

words & pictures

It's a bit dull out there today—the kind of weather that makes you want to stay inside.

But I'm sooo bored!
I've already done some playing, reading, coloring, drawing, and gluing...I don't know what to do now.

GO AND PLAY OUTSIDE, SWEETHEART,
BUT BE CAREFUL—AND DON'T GO TOO FAR!

The street is empty.

Well, not quite...

I turn around and see a funny shape getting closer.

A ball of fur wearing a pink hat goes past on a tiny bike.

He looks at me.

I hop on my bike and follow him...

...and off we go!

ZIP

HEY!

WAIT FOR ME!

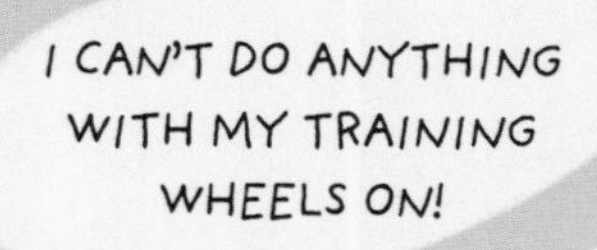
I CAN'T DO ANYTHING
WITH MY TRAINING
WHEELS ON!

SHOW OFF!

GRRRRR

I'VE HAD ENOUGH!
I WANT TO TAKE
MY TRAINING WHEELS OFF!

SPLAT!

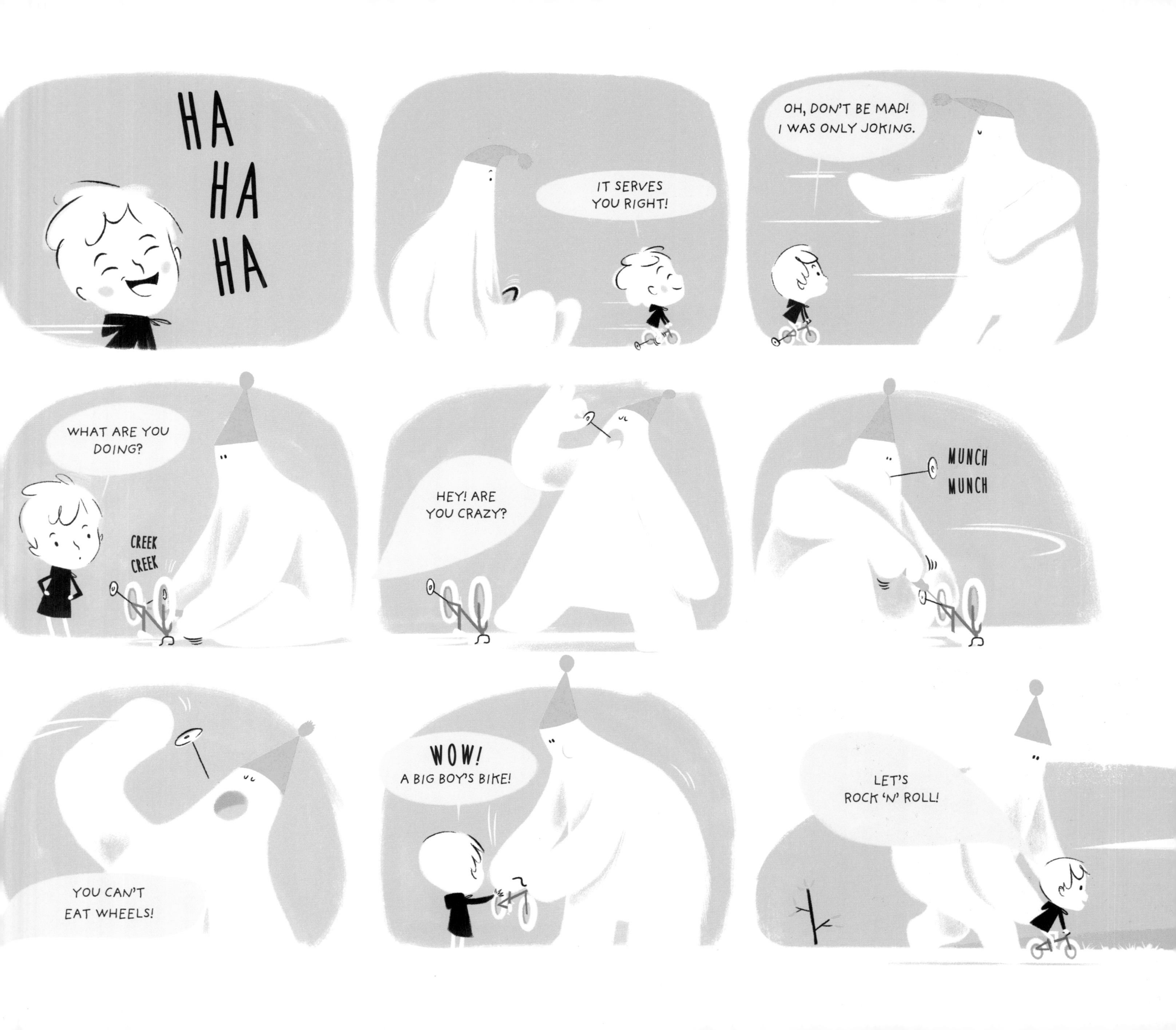
HA
HA
HA
IT SERVES YOU RIGHT!
OH, DON'T BE MAD! I WAS ONLY JOKING.
WHAT ARE YOU DOING?
CREEK
CREEK
HEY! ARE YOU CRAZY?
MUNCH
MUNCH
YOU CAN'T EAT WHEELS!
WOW!
A BIG BOY'S BIKE!
LET'S ROCK 'N' ROLL!

I like feeling the wind on my face.

He stands behind me.

Tall.

Strong.

Friendly.

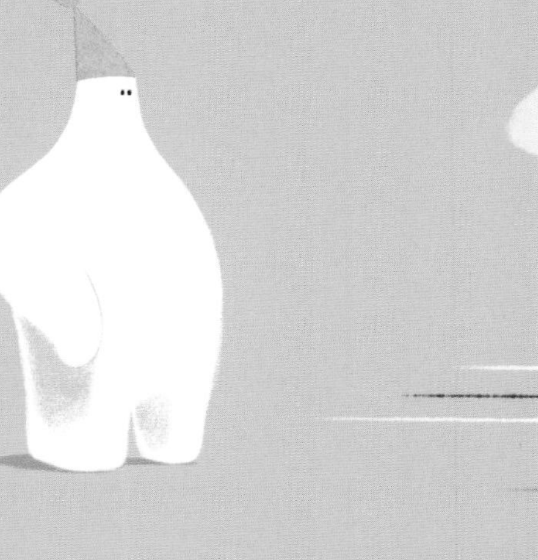
OH!

OH DEAR!
IT'S NOT EASY!

AHHHH!

WAHHHH!

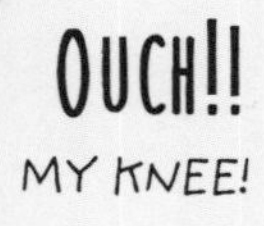
OUCH!!
MY KNEE!

BOO
HOO

MUCH BETTER
WITH A HUG.

WHAT ARE
YOU DOING?

OUCHEY!
PSCHHHHH

A BANDAGE!
HOORAY!

SMACK!

CHOCOLATE!!

YUM
YUM

After all the excitement,
we deserve a little rest.
A ray of sun gently warms us
as the river lulls us to sleep.

OK!
HERE WE GO AGAIN.
YOU HOLD ON TO ME, RIGHT?

PHEW!
NOT SO FAAAAAAAST!

ZOOOOM
HELP!

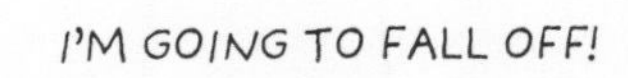

I'M GOING TO FALL OFF!
WOBBLE WOBBLE
WOOOOOAH!

BAM!

I'M TOO WOBBLY!

BAM!

THAT'S OK,
YOU CAN LET ME GO NOW.

HEY!

AT LAST, I GET IT! I JUST NEED
TO LOOK STRAIGHT AHEAD.

Here we go!

Now, I'm riding at the front.

I'm sooo happy.

I go faster...

...except I don't know how to use the brakes yet!

WHEEEEE

I'M GOING TOO FAST.

AAAAH
SPLAT

HA HA HA
DIDN'T FEEL A THING.

IT'S MY BIKE THAT NEEDS A BANDAGE THIS TIME.

CLIC CLAC

PSCHOOT PSCHOOT

OH NO, IT'S RAINING...
PITAPAT PITAPAT

I THINK HE KNOWS WHAT TO DO.

FLFFFF
CRACK
YOUR UMBRELLA IS BROKEN!
IT'S TOO SLIPPERY. WE NEED TO STOP!
WE COULD HAVE FALLEN AND HURT OUR HEADS.
COOL! A RED HELMET, JUST LIKE MY BIKE.
I WON'T BE SCARED ANYMORE, EVEN WHEN YOU'RE NOT AROUND.
LET'S GO AGAIN!
DO YOU WANT TO RACE??!

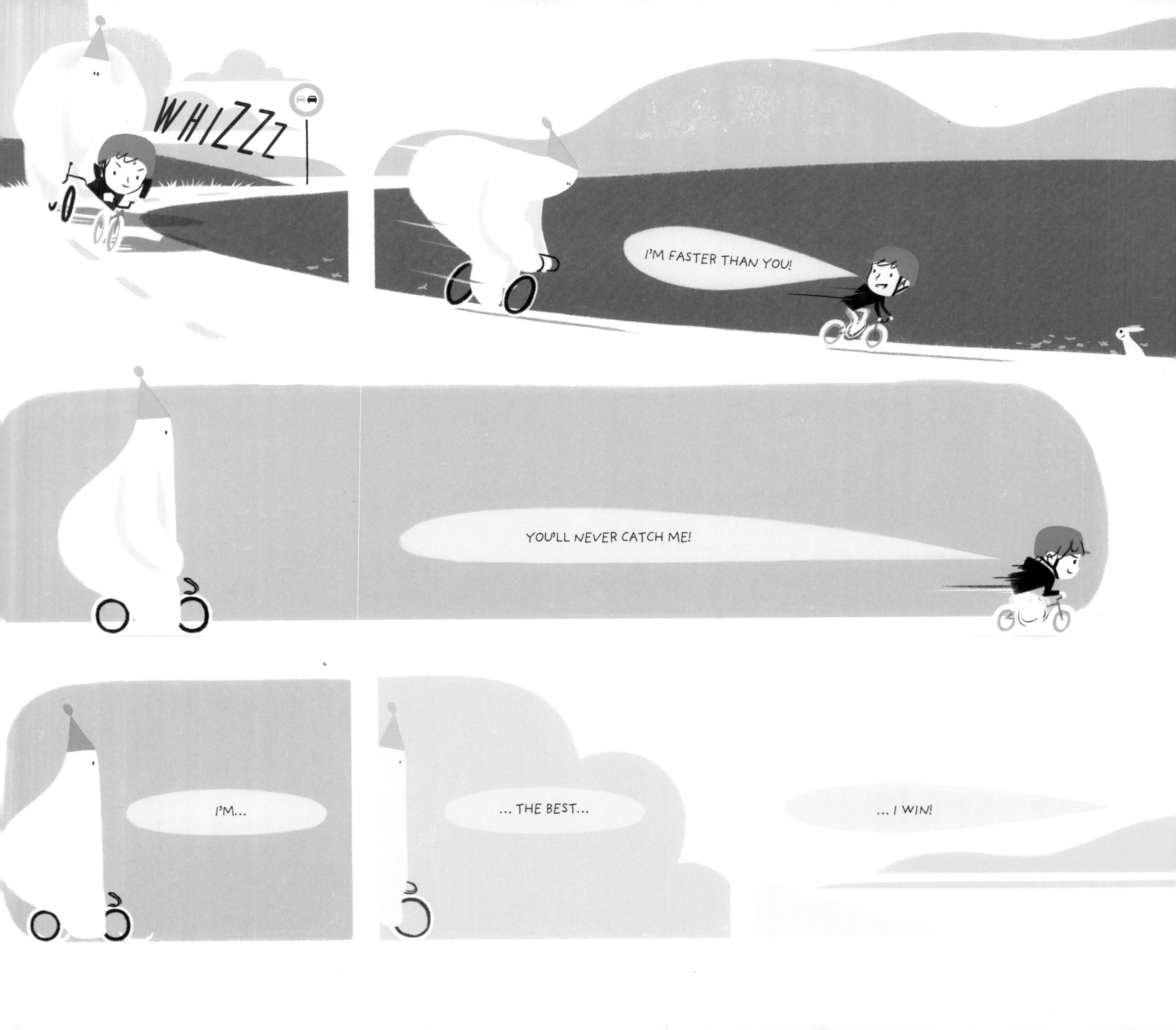
WHIZZZz
I'M FASTER THAN YOU!
YOU'LL NEVER CATCH ME!
I'M...
... THE BEST...
... I WIN!

When I turn around,
I'm all by myself—he's gone.
I feel lost.

And a bit scared.
But I look straight ahead
like he showed me.
I know the way.

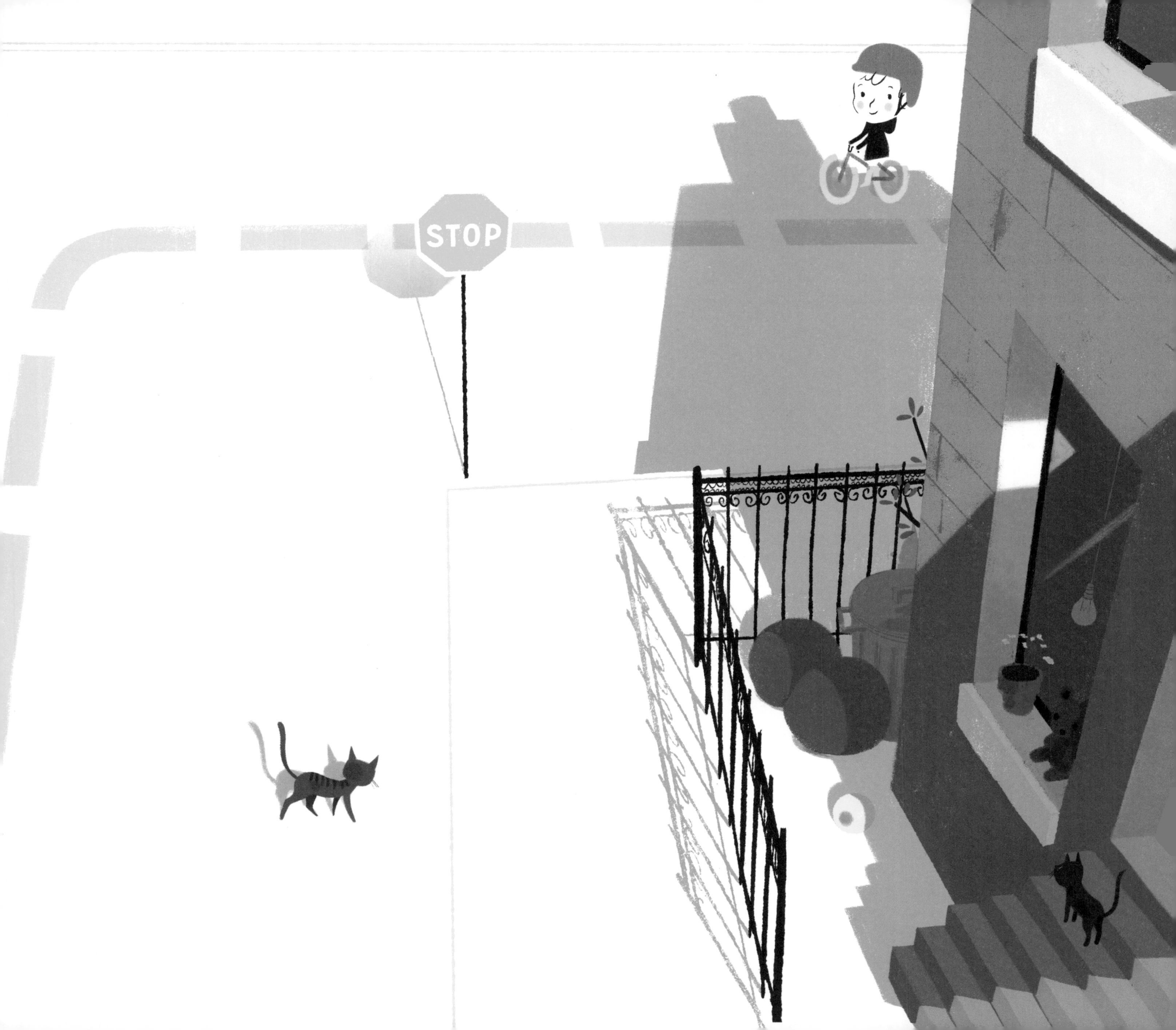

STOP

Now the sun is shining.
I take all the time in the world to get home.
I feel a bit sad, but also proud.
I really want to tell Mom and Dad,
but who'll believe that a ball of fur in a pink hat
ate my training wheels?

I put my bike down carefully.
With my helmet on my head and a bandage on my knee,
I feel like a big boy now.

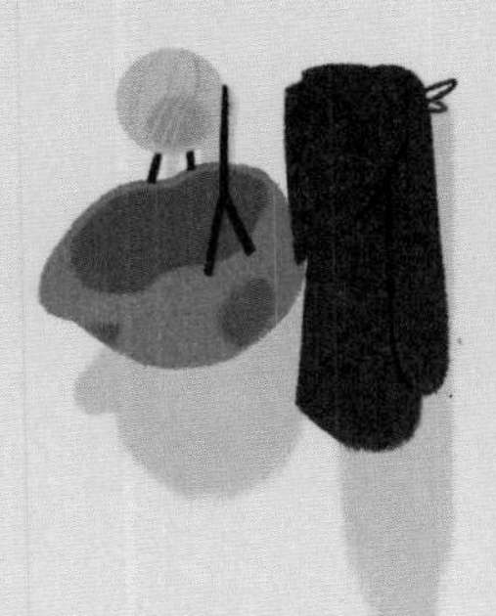

MOM, I'M HOME!
THAT'S GREAT, SWEETHEART—
WHAT DID YOU DO?
OH, UM, NOTHING MUCH—
I JUST WENT FOR A RIDE...

END

Certificate for a

SUPER CYCLIST

On ..../........../..........,
you took your training wheels off.
You can now ride a bike
like a big boy/girl!

CONGRATULATIONS!